Anderson University Library

D1048589

S

Amazing
Stories

★ ★ ★ ★ ★ ★

OTHER YEARLING BOOKS YOU WILL ENJOY:

BABE RUTH AND THE HOME RUN DERBY
(ALL-STAR MEATBALLS #1), Stephen Mooser
THE TERRIBLE TICKLER
(ALL-STAR MEATBALLS #2), Stephen Mooser
SCARY SCRAPED-UP SKATERS
(ALL-STAR MEATBALLS #3), Stephen Mooser
THE HEADLESS SNOWMAN
(ALL-STAR MEATBALLS #4), Stephen Mooser
THE SNOW BOWL
(ALL-STAR MEATBALLS #5), Stephen Mooser
MUSCLE MANIA
(ALL-STAR MEATBALLS #6), Stephen Mooser
IT'S A WEIRD, WEIRD SCHOOL, Stephen Mooser
THE HITCHHIKING VAMPIRE, Stephen Mooser
DUMP DAYS, Jerry Spinelli
BOBBY BASEBALL, Robert Kimmel Smith

YEARLING BOOKS/YOUNG YEARLINGS/YEARLING CLASSICS are designed especially to entertain and enlighten young people. Patricia Reilly Giff, consultant to this series, received her bachelor's degree from Marymount College and a master's degree in history from St. John's University. She holds a Professional Diploma in Reading and a Doctorate of Humane Letters from Hofstra University. She was a teacher and reading consultant for many years, and is the author of numerous books for young readers.

For a complete listing of all Yearling titles,
write to
Dell Readers Service,
P.O. Box 1045,
South Holland, IL 60473.

ALL-STAR MEATBALLS #7

Amazing
Stories

★ ★ ★ ★ ★ ★

STEPHEN MOOSER

**Illustrated by
GEORGE ULRICH**

A YEARLING BOOK

Published by
Dell Publishing
a division of
Bantam Doubleday Dell Publishing Group, Inc.
666 Fifth Avenue
New York, New York 10103

If you purchased this book without a cover you should be aware that this book is stolen property. It was reported as "unsold and destroyed" to the publisher and neither the author nor the publisher has received any payment for this "stripped book."

Text copyright © 1993 by Stephen Mooser
Illustrations copyright © 1993 by George Ulrich

All rights reserved. No part of this book may be reproduced or transmitted in any form or by any means, electronic or mechanical, including photocopying, recording, or by any information storage and retrieval system, without the written permission of the Publisher, except where permitted by law.

The trademark Yearling® is registered in the U.S. Patent and Trademark Office.

The trademark Dell® is registered in the U.S. Patent and Trademark Office.

ISBN: 0-440-40646-3

Printed in the United States of America

February 1993

10 9 8 7 6 5 4 3 2 1

OPM

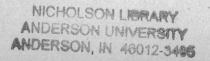
NICHOLSON LIBRARY
ANDERSON UNIVERSITY
ANDERSON, IN 46012-3495

For the amazing Ginsburg kids:
Leah, Michael, Sarah, Jacob, and Marco

JUV
PZ
7
.M78817
AMA
1993

NICHOLSON LIBRARY
ANDERSON UNIVERSITY
ANDERSON IN 46012-3495

CONTENTS

LIST OF CHARACTERS

They're hilarious, they're strange, and even though they're not jocks, they are into sports. Here's the All-Star Meatballs starting lineup:

HOMER KING: He's been seen at Bayview School in his pajama top and also in his underwear, but he's best known for his skill at hitting home runs and throwing meatballs.

MOLLY JAMES: She's got a bow in her hair the size of a TV antenna and a dog named Godzilla that only she can see.

DARRYL PUMPWATER: He's got the whole Meatballs Club groaning, but not because his clothes are on inside out and backwards. It's because no one can bear his corny jokes.

KATE BARNETT: She can see things better than anyone, even though she's blind.

NICOLE MARTIN: She can dance, play football, and roller-skate too. She's easy to spot: there's a ponytail shooting from the top of her head like a hairy fountain.

xi

LUIS CRUZON: He can walk across a tightrope, juggle a fishbowl, and balance a birthday cake on his head. Pretty special tricks, especially for a boy with only one arm.

And let's not forget . . .

MR. FOSTER: Before he became the Meatballs' teacher, he was a monkey trainer in the circus. He believes that students, like monkeys, learn best when a banana is the reward. A bunch hangs above his desk.

MAXIE BUTTS: He's big, mean, and full of nasty tricks. He and his gang, the Jokers, don't get along with the Meatballs. Not one bit.

BILLY TUBBS: He's Maxie's best friend, skinny as a scarecrow and just as handsome.

CHAPTER 1

Ghost Story

"PIRATE TREASURE!" shouted Darryl Pumpwater, bursting into class one Monday morning. "I know where we can dig up a skeleton stuffed with gold!"

Mr. Foster looked up from his desk.

"Please take your seat," he said. "It's eight o'clock. Time to begin."

As usual Darryl looked as if he'd been dressed by a tornado. His pants were on inside out. His T-shirt was on backwards. His cap was on inside out AND backwards.

"I'm serious," he said. He stretched out his hands to the class. "You've got to believe me. The body of Captain Golden Guts is buried right here in Bayview!"

Only Homer King seemed to be listening to Darryl. His eyes were as round as the blue polka dots on his too-big T-shirt. His mouth was flopped open like an oven door. No one else was paying the slightest attention. They were either reading, or drawing, or talking to their neighbors.

Mr. Foster had a bushy mustache and a warm smile. "Darryl, please," he said. "Take your seat."

"Just before the pirate was killed he hid all his gold coins by eating them!" exclaimed Darryl. "Just this morning I found out where he's planted. Down at the beach!"

"Wow!" said Homer.

2

"Darryl, please. We have a lot to cover today," said Mr. Foster.

"After school I'm going to the beach to dig up his bones," said Darryl. "Wowie, cowie, zowie! By tomorrow I'll be a zillionaire!"

"That's very nice," said Mr. Foster. He pointed to Darryl's desk at the back of the room.

Darryl waved a scrap of paper at the class. "I even have a map!"

Molly James was quietly petting her pretend poodle, Godzilla. Luis Cruzon yawned, then put his head down on his desk. The rest of the class waited for Mr. Foster to begin the lesson.

Homer leaned halfway out of his chair trying to read Darryl's map.

"Darryl, we're waiting," said Mr. Foster.

Darryl shook his head and started down the aisle. "Doesn't anyone believe me?" he asked.

"No!" everyone shouted back. Everyone

but Homer. He was licking his lips and furiously writing in his notebook.

Darryl tossed the map onto his desk. Then he slid into his seat, lowered his head, and sulked.

"No one believes you because you're always joking and making up stories," said Mr. Foster. "We never know what's the truth and what isn't."

"It's all the truth," said Darryl, loudly tapping his finger on the desk. "Well, okay. Maybe sometimes I exaggerate. A little."

"A little!" said Nicole Martin, turning around in her desk. There was a ponytail sprouting from the top of her head, like a hairy fountain. "You exaggerate all the time."

"Like when?" said Darryl.

"Like when you said you were going to be a major-league pitcher. Like when you said Martians took you for a ride in their flying saucer. Or when you said you'd win that giant ruby they're giving away at Ruby's Donuts."

"I am going to win that ruby," said Darryl. "Mr. Chamberlain at the donut shop announced that the company has hidden a ruby in a bag of donut holes. Sometime before Valentine's Day someone is going to win it."

"Yeah, but there are thousands of Ruby's Donuts shops all over the world," said Molly. "The chances of you getting the ruby are a million to one."

"The way I figure it, the odds are more like two million to one," said Kate Barnett. Kate was blind. She was also the smartest student in class. "That's almost no chance at all."

"So?" said Darryl. "If you want to win, you can't give up just because the odds are bad. Champions aren't quitters."

Mr. Foster smiled. "How would you like to be a champion this week?"

"Of what?" asked Darryl.

"Friday morning at eight there will be a tall tale contest in the auditorium," said Mr. Foster. "The class that comes up with the tallest tale wins a trip to Paul Bunyan Land."

"Wowie, cowie, kablowie!" said Darryl. "That place is great!"

"They have the best rides anywhere," said Molly. There was a bow in her hair as big as a TV antenna.

"They have the Tornado Twister," said Nicole. "That thing is scary!"

"I'd rather go on the merry-go-round," said Homer. He looked at Molly and blushed. "Someday I'm going to ride it with my special valentine."

The class giggled. They knew how much Homer liked Molly. Probably more than she liked him.

Luis only had one arm. He raised it high over his head. "How do we enter the contest?" he asked.

"It's easy," said Mr. Foster. "Each class

thinks up a tall tale and then tells it on Friday morning. The best story wins the tickets."

"What's a tall tale?" asked Darryl. "Is it a story about basketball players? Or about the Empire State Building? Or about climbing Mount Everest?"

"Tall tales are exaggerated stories," explained Mr. Foster. "They're about winds strong enough to blow the paint off a house. About people so fast, they can run into the future. Or about giant lumberjacks, like Paul Bunyan, who could rip up trees with their bare hands."

"When I get bigger I'll be able to do that too," said Darryl. He stood up and made a muscle. "In fact, I'm going to be so big, I'll use the trees for toothpicks."

"I don't see how this class can lose," said Mr. Foster. "Darryl is the greatest teller of tall tales in the whole school."

"Hey, my stories are all true," said Darryl, slapping his chest.

"Please," cried the class. "On Friday tell the story of Captain Golden Guts. Send us to Paul Bunyan Land."

Darryl shrugged his shoulders and slumped back into his seat. "I couldn't tell the story of Golden Guts. It's not a tall tale." He lowered his head. "Besides, it scares me to give a speech."

"C'mon, Darryl," begged the class.

Mr. Foster patted a clump of bananas hanging above his desk. "Maybe one of these will change your mind. If you tell your story at the assembly, I'll give you a banana."

Before coming to Bayview School, Mr. Foster had taught tricks to monkeys in the circus. He still believed that children, like monkeys, performed best when a banana was the reward.

"Sorry. I just can't. What if people laugh?" said Darryl. He put his hands over his face and shuddered. Just thinking about speaking in public made him shake.

The last time he had spoken had been in kindergarten, and it had turned out horrible. Really embarrassing.

"You don't need to worry. No one will laugh at you," said Mr. Foster.

"It doesn't matter anyway," said Darryl. "By Friday I'll be on my way to California. After school today I'm trying out for the Angels."

"The California Angels!" gasped Homer. "The major-league baseball team?"

"Yep!" said Darryl, sitting up tall. "An Angels scout is coming here after school. I think they may want me to pitch for them this year." He looked around the room. "Why don't the rest of you Meatballs try out too?"

Homer, Luis, Molly, Nicole, and Kate were, like Darryl, all members of the Meatballs Club. They had gotten their strange name the first day of school, after they had started a meatball fight in the cafeteria against the Jokers gang. The Jokers and the Meatballs still didn't get along. Especially since Homer had beaten them later that week in the Home Run Derby.

"I love the Angels," said Luis. "They have a one-handed pitcher."

"Maybe I could play for them too," said Homer.

"They'll pick you for sure," said Darryl. "You're the Home Run Derby champ."

"We'd be teammates!" said Homer. He put his hands behind his head and leaned back in his chair, dreaming.

"Homer, you're such a sucker," said Molly. "No scout is coming to Bayview School. This is just another one of Darryl's tall tales."

Darryl turned and glared. "All right, Molly James, just for that you're not getting any of Captain Golden Guts's treasure."

CHAPTER 2

The Head Scout

AFTER SCHOOL, Homer and Darryl hiked out to the ball field. It was February, but spring was already in the air. Leaves were blooming on the trees, grass was sprouting on the field, and everything smelled new and sweet.

"This better not be another one of your made-up stories," said Homer, hurrying to keep up with Darryl. "I still remember that

13

freezing night we waited in your backyard for the flying saucer. The one that was going to take us to Mars."

Darryl shrugged. "Don't blame me for that. Blame the Martians. They're the ones who forgot my address."

Homer sighed. "Come on, Darryl. Admit it. Sometimes you make things up."

Darryl pretended not to hear. But he knew that Homer was right. He did like to exaggerate. He wanted people to think he was special.

"Hey, we're right on time," said Darryl. He pointed to a clump of kids in the middle of the field. They were standing around a skinny man in a red baseball cap. "Look. There's the scout now."

Homer squinted. "How come all those kids with him are kindergartners?"

"I don't know. But I'm not complaining," said Darryl. He slapped Homer on the back. "Beating out those shrimps will be super easy."

14

Homer took an old comb out of his pocket.

"I hope I don't mess up," he said, nervously combing his wavy red hair. "Look who's standing by the backstop. It's Maxie Butts and his gang, the Jokers."

"Hey, Meatballs!" cried Maxie. He was wearing coveralls and sharp-pointed cowboy boots. "Are you going to be Angels?"

Darryl and Homer didn't reply.

"They'll never pick them!" shouted Maxie's best friend, Billy Tubbs. Billy had a long face and a ton of teeth. He was wearing a duck-billed baseball cap, turned backwards.

"I wonder why they're not trying out too?" said Homer.

"Probably too chicken," said Darryl.

The man in the red cap had just finished explaining something when Darryl and Homer walked up.

"Excuse me," said Darryl, raising his hand. "Is this for the Angels?"

"That's right," said the man, smiling. He reached over the crowd with a long arm. "I'm Reggie Downs, head scout."

"Wowie cowie," said Darryl. He turned to Homer. "Did you hear that? Head scout!"

Homer gulped. Then combed faster.

"Let's spread out," said Mr. Downs. "Form a circle. Grab hands."

Everyone made a big circle. Darryl took the hand of a little girl with twin ponytails. A kindergartner with a muddy nose took Homer's hand and they all made a circle.

"Around and around we go!" said Mr. Downs, standing in the center, waving his arms. "Dance!"

"What kind of a tryout is this?" asked Homer, shuffling around the ring.

"It's a major-league warm-up exercise," said Darryl. "Don't you know anything?"

"I know that the Jokers are laughing and pointing," said Homer, nodding toward the backstop. "I feel silly."

"Now sing!" said Mr. Downs, waving his arms like a conductor. "Ring around the rosy, a pocketful of posy. Ashes! Ashes! All fall down!"

Everyone fell to the grass. Homer and Darryl too.

The Jokers grabbed their sides and laughed.

Homer sat up and glared at Darryl. "Are you sure this is what they do in the big leagues?"

"I think so," said Darryl, getting up.

"Now let's play patty-cake!" said Mr. Downs, clapping his hands. "Grab a partner. Let's have some fun!"

"Patty-cake?" said Homer.

"Time out!" said Darryl, making a *T* with his hands. He squinted at Mr. Downs. "Are you really from the California Angels?"

"The baseball team?" asked Mr. Downs.

"Of course," said Darryl.

The man laughed. "I don't know any-

17

NICHOLSON LIBRARY
ANDERSON UNIVERSITY
ANDERSON, IN 46012-3495

thing about baseball. I'm with the Angel Scouts. We're a kindergarten club."

Homer groaned and shut his eyes. "I should have known," he muttered.

Just then the Jokers came strutting over, laughing.

"You Meatballs are such sillies," said Maxie. He was missing his two front teeth. Each *s* came out like a hiss.

"Go on. Play patty-cake. We want to watch," said the Jokers. They were all crowded behind Maxie, pointing and giggling.

"Make like a rocket, Butts. Take off," said Homer, trying to sound tough.

Just then the boy with the muddy nose grabbed Homer's hand. "Will you be my patty-cake partner? Will you?"

"No," whispered Homer, his face turning as red as his hair. "Not now."

The Jokers laughed and played patty-cake with each other.

"This is all your fault!" said Homer, angrily turning on Darryl. "You twisted up the whole story about the Angels."

"You do tell some wild stories," said Maxie. He stepped forward and slapped Darryl on the shoulder. "I hope you're not planning to tell any of them at the Tall Tale Contest."

"Maxie told us about the last time you gave a speech, in kindergarten," said Billy. "What a laugh!"

Darryl glared at Billy. Maybe Billy and the Jokers thought it was funny. But it was the most embarrassing thing that had ever happened.

"His pants were on backwards," said Maxie, pointing at Darryl. "And his fly was open."

"When he turned around, everyone could see his red underpants!" said Billy, finishing the story.

"We laughed so hard, I thought the walls would come down," said Maxie.

"It wasn't funny," muttered Darryl, lowering his eyes. "It was embarrassing. I've been afraid to give a speech ever since."

"Maxie is winning us those tickets to Paul Bunyan Land," said Billy. "He's going to tell the tallest tale ever. It's all about the make-believe pirate, Captain Golden Guts."

BLAM! Maxie slapped Billy on the shoulder. "What's wrong with you, Tubbs! Do you want the Meatballs to steal my story?"

"Your story!" said Homer. "That's Darryl's story. He's going to tell it."

"He'd better not," said Maxie.

"I already told everyone I'm not giving any speeches," said Darryl. "Besides, it's no tall tale. And tomorrow I'll dig up that gold and prove it."

The Jokers laughed.

"You'll never get any treasure. You'll never even get that Valentine's ruby they're giving away at the donut shop,"

said Maxie. "I see you down there every morning."

"I'll win it. You'll see," said Darryl.

"Darryl is going to be rich," said Homer.

"Another tall tale," said Billy.

"Take my advice," said Maxie. He put a finger against Darryl's forehead. "Don't enter that contest. Or else!"

"Or else what?" said Darryl.

"Or else this!" said Maxie. He shoved Darryl in the chest with both hands. Darryl toppled backwards and fell over one of the Jokers, who was crouching right behind him.

"Hey! Whoa!" yelled Darryl.

WHAM! He landed on his back.

"Ouch!"

"He went upside down! Just like you do on the Tornado Twister at Paul Bunyan Land!" said Maxie, pointing.

The Jokers howled. They slapped each other on the hands then walked away, poking each other in the sides and laughing.

Darryl sat up and rubbed his back. "Someday those guys will be sorry. Real sorry."

"Beat them at the Tall Tale Contest," said Homer. "That will show them."

"I'm not entering any tall tale contest," said Darryl. "I told you a zillion times. I'm not going to let Maxie make fun of me again like he did in kindergarten." He stared off at Maxie and his gang. "I'll get back at them, though. No problem. I'll get my friends from Mars to zap them with their ray guns."

CHAPTER 3

Meatball Tales

Tuesday morning, before school, Darryl went to Ruby's Donuts and bought a bag of donut holes. Then he hurried out and looked inside the bag for the big prize, the giant ruby. It wasn't there, again.

"Rats," he said, leaning against the wall outside the shop. "I have the worst luck."

Darryl ate some of the donut holes. The

rest he threw to a flock of pigeons gathered on the sidewalk.

"Hi," said Homer, coming by on his way to school. He was with two other Meatballs, Kate and Molly.

Kate sniffed the air. Even though she was blind, she usually knew everything that was going on.

"How are those donuts?" she asked.

"Ask the pigeons," said Darryl. "They like them better than I do. I'm only after that jewel."

"What if you find it?" asked Molly. There was a polka-dotted bow in her hair as big as a satellite dish. "What will you do with the money?"

"Buy Maxie a one-way ticket to the South Pole," said Darryl. "That way he won't bug me anymore."

"You have to stand up to him. Otherwise he'll never stop," said Molly. "Just beat him at that contest on Friday. Show him you're not afraid."

26

Everyone started toward school. Darryl kicked a rock along the sidewalk and thought about what Molly had said.

"After school we're meeting at the Meatballs Clubhouse," said Molly. "We'll work on our tall tale. You need to help us think one up. Then you can tell it at the assembly."

Darryl shivered. Just thinking about standing up in front of the school made him dizzy. "I can't. I'm sorry."

"What do you mean, you can't?" said Molly. She stopped and shook her finger in Darryl's face. "Give me one good reason why the greatest teller of tall tales can't help us out."

"Umm . . . ummm," said Darryl, biting his lip. "Umm . . . I told you I don't tell tall tales. They're all true."

Molly shook her head. The giant bow in her hair brushed against Darryl's nose. "All right, then. Tell one of your true stories. We'll just say it's made up."

"Umm . . . ummm," said Darryl, biting his thumb, "I—I can't do that either."

"But you have to," said Homer. "I want to go to Paul Bunyan Land. So does Molly. She wants to go on a special ride with me."

Molly raised an eyebrow. "I do?"

Homer blushed.

Darryl shook his head. "I'm sorry," he whispered. "I can't. Speeches scare me."

After school everyone went to the Meatballs Clubhouse. It was in a room at the back of TV Channel Six. Before becoming their clubhouse it had been the set of the TV sports show *Kenny's Krazy Korner*. The Meatballs had won the clubhouse in a football game against the Jokers.

When Darryl walked in, everyone was already there. Molly and Kate were sitting on a long brown couch shaped like a hollowed-out football. Homer and Luis were sitting in fat chairs shaped like baseball mitts, and Nicole was standing next to a lamp made out of a hockey stick, with a basketball hoop for a shade. She had a pad of paper and a pen in one hand. She reached up and wiggled her fountain of hair with her other hand.

"Will the meeting please come to order," she said. "It's time to think up a tall tale." She held up the notepad. "I'll write down all your suggestions. But please, don't shout them all out at once."

No one shouted anything. Silence filled the room. Then Luis coughed. Homer cracked his knuckles. Darryl started to hum.

Nicole sighed. "All right. I'll start. My tall tale is about a woman with the strongest stomach in the world. She eats snails!"

"That's not a tall tale," said Homer. "My father eats snails all the time. They serve them at French restaurants."

"Oh," said Nicole, crossing out the story. "Anyone else?"

"How about a person so smart they get all A's," said Homer. "That's a good tall tale."

"That is a good story," said Nicole, writing it down. "We'll call it 'The Smartest Person in the World.' "

"That isn't a tall tale either," said Kate. "I get all A's. And I'm not even the smartest person in the world."

"Oh," said Nicole, erasing her words.

"I've got a story," said Luis, raising his hand. "It's about a person who could hit a baseball fifty miles!"

Kate touched the single freckle at the tip of her nose. "Bingo!" she said. "That's a tall tale for sure."

Nicole started to write, *The Best Hitter Ever—*"

"My brother hit a baseball a thousand miles," said Homer. "Really."

"He did not," said Luis.

"Yes, he did," said Homer. "He hit a ball that landed in the back of a truck going by. The truck ended up traveling to Chicago. That's over a thousand miles away."

"Rats!" said Nicole, crossing out the story. "We'll never make up a tall tale. We'll never get to Paul Bunyan Land."

"Not without Darryl," said Molly. "Please. Just tell one of your stories on Friday."

Darryl was scrunched down in the corner of the big couch. "I can't," he said softly. "Everyone will laugh if I come out onstage." He pulled his inside-out cap down over his eyes. "Please. Don't make me."

Molly clucked her tongue and shook her head.

"I know a tall tale," she said. "It's about the biggest chicken in the world."

"Great!" said Nicole, furiously scribbling away. "Does he lay the biggest egg in the world?"

"No," said Molly. She glared at Darryl. "He doesn't lay eggs. He just *lays* around, doing nothing. Worst of all, he's too chicken to help his friends."

CHAPTER 4

Bones!

ON WEDNESDAY Darryl came to school with a shovel.

"I'm going to dig up Captain Golden Guts after school," he announced, sliding the shovel under the coatrack. "If anyone wants to get rich, you can come along."

"I'll come!" said Homer, raising his hand.

"Homer, you're such a sucker," said

Molly. There was a red bow atop her head as big as the Valentine's heart in the window of Sprague's Card Shop. She pointed it at Darryl. "If there really was a skeleton at the beach, Darryl wouldn't go near it. He'd be too scared."

Homer gulped. He reached into the pocket of his too-long striped pants, got out his comb, and started combing his wavy red hair. "That skeleton couldn't hurt us. Could it?"

"Of course not," said Molly. "Because there is no skeleton. It's just a tall tale."

"And a good one too," said Mr. Foster. "I bet it wins us those tickets on Friday."

Homer reached across the aisle and tapped Molly on the shoulder. "When we go to Paul Bunyan Land we can go on a ride together, for Valentine's."

"We'll see," said Molly.

Homer grinned. "She said yes! Sort of," he whispered, looking down at his desk and blushing.

"Darryl's story isn't going to win us anything," said Luis. "I heard that Maxie Butts is telling the story of Captain Golden Guts. And since Maxie's last name begins with *B,* he'll get to go on first."

"Then Darryl will just have to think up another story," said Mr. Foster. He patted the bananas hanging above his desk. "Don't forget the special bonus I'm offering."

Darryl didn't care about Mr. Foster's bananas. He wasn't even paying attention. He was staring out the window and dreaming about the gold inside the moldy ribs of Captain Golden Guts.

If I can get that gold, I'll take everyone to Paul Bunyan Land, he thought, closing his eyes. *That way I won't have to speak at the assembly. But everyone will still like me.*

After school Homer and Darryl walked down to the beach. Darryl was carrying his shovel over his shoulder like a soldier. Homer was combing his hair.

"Sometimes pirate treasure is haunted," said Homer. "What if we dig up a ghost?"

"All we're going to dig up is gold," said Darryl. He tipped his inside-out cap. "Trust me. I know what I'm doing."

"That's what you said about the Martians. That's what you said about the Angels," said Homer. He stopped and looked Darryl up and down. "This better not be a tall tale."

"No way," said Darryl. "It's the truth. My cousin told me about it. He's in high school."

"Oh," said Homer, nodding. "An expert."

The treasure hunters marched down Main Street, past the ballet studio, the roller rink, and Ruby's Donuts. Then they crossed Cottage Street, cut through the alley behind the market, and arrived at the beach.

It was a damp, chilly day. The air was filled with the smell of salt water, seaweed, and the cries of seagulls. Except for a fisherman standing in the surf and a bunch of kids playing football, the beach was deserted.

Darryl looked around to make sure no one was watching. Then he took out his crumpled map and opened it up.

"I drew this after I talked to my cousin," he whispered, showing it to Homer. He pointed to a big X he'd made. It was halfway between the parking lot and the ocean. Darryl looked back at the parking lot. Then he headed for the water, silently counting his steps.

"How do you know this is where he's buried?" asked Homer, hurrying alongside. "I don't think the parking lot was here when Captain Golden Guts died. Cars weren't even invented yet."

Darryl rolled his eyes. "Of course cars weren't invented. But there was still a

parking lot. It's where the pirates used to park their horses."

"It was?" said Homer. He tilted his head. "I thought pirates traveled on ships."

Darryl came to a halt, looked at the map one last time, then turned to Homer and sighed. "Do you want to look for the gold or not? If you don't want to be a zillionaire, that's okay with me."

"I was just wondering, that's all," said Homer.

"Stop wondering. Start digging," said Darryl. He handed Homer the shovel. "According to my cousin we're standing right over the rotting ribs of old Golden Guts."

"We are?" said Homer. He threw down the shovel and leapt to the side. "Eee-yikes!"

Darryl clucked his tongue. "Those bones can't hurt us," he said. He pointed to the place where Homer had been standing. "Now come on. Dig."

Homer got out his comb and ran it through his hair. "Maybe we ought to leave that gold alone," he said. "What if there's a curse on it?"

"There's no such thing as curses," said Darryl. But deep down he wasn't so sure. He felt like he was cursed himself. Years ago Maxie had put a spell on him to keep him from speaking in public. A spell he couldn't seem to break.

Homer put away his comb and picked up the shovel. "Okay," he said. "But what if we don't find anything?"

"Don't worry. We will," said Darryl.

Homer gulped.

"Just dig," said Darryl.

And he did.

The sand flew. Little by little the hole grew bigger and deeper. After about fifteen minutes Homer stopped and Darryl took over.

"I can almost smell the treasure," said Darryl, stepping into the hole. "Soon we'll be so rich, we can take the whole class to Paul Bunyan Land."

"We'll be so rich, we can buy Paul Bunyan Land!" said Homer, rubbing his hands. "Molly and I can ride the merry-go-round all day on Valentine's!"

Darryl looked up from the hole and put a finger to his lips. "Keep your voice down," he said. "We don't want anyone to know we're here digging up old Golden Guts."

Suddenly a shower of sand came raining down on Darryl and Homer.

"Hey!" said Darryl whipping around. "Who's—"

WHAP! Another handful of sand stung him in the face.

"Stop it!" said Homer. "You could hurt his eyes!"

Darryl shook the sand from his cap and looked up at Maxie Butts and the Jokers. Maxie grinned, showing off his missing teeth.

"We were just playing football down the beach," he said. "The Jokers and I thought maybe you might need some help."

"Take a walk, Maxie," said Darryl. He went back to his digging. "Can't you see we're busy?"

"You're wasting your time," said Billy Tubbs. He picked at his teeth with his thumbnail. "If you want to know the real story about Golden Guts, listen to Maxie on Friday."

"You guys are such suckers," hissed Maxie. "Don't you know that the story of Golden Guts is just a tall tale?"

Darryl bit his lip and dug faster.

"Leave us alone," said Homer, scrunching up his face. His shoes were overflowing with sand. So were the cuffs of his oversized pants. "We know what we're doing. Don't we, Darryl?"

"Ooooh, look," said Maxie, pointing. "Darryl has his pants on backwards. His fly is open!"

"Huh?" said Darryl. He reached back and felt the back of his pants. They were on right. Maxie was just making fun.

Darryl closed his eyes. Then started digging again. "Someday, when I'm rich, you'll be sorry," he muttered.

Suddenly another shower of sand came raining down on Darryl and Homer.

"Quit it!" said Homer, shutting his eyes.

"Oh, my!" said Darryl, spotting something in the sand. He dropped his shovel and got down on his knees. The Jokers laughed and launched another load of sand.

"Wowie, cowie, kablowie!" shouted Darryl, as the sand rained down like hail. "Bones!"

CHAPTER 5

More Bones

DARRYL THRUST his hand into the air.

"We're rich!" he screamed.

Everyone gasped. A bone the size of a ruler was clasped tightly in his fist.

Homer gulped and reached for his comb.

"Believe me now?" said Darryl, digging away with his hands, like a dog chasing a

47

gopher. "I knew Captain Golden Guts wasn't a tall tale."

"We knew it," said Homer, peering cautiously into the pit. "You shouldn't have laughed."

Maxie held out his arms. "We weren't laughing," he said. "I hope you're planning to share that gold. We helped you find it."

"How? By throwing sand?"

"We weren't throwing sand. We were digging," said Billy. He got down on his knees and squinted into the pit. "See any treasure?"

"It can't be far now," said Darryl. He threw a handful of bones out of the pit. "No doubt about it. These are ribs."

Everyone looked at the bones, then quickly turned away.

"Gross," said Billy.

"I hope you don't find his skull," said Homer. He was combing so fast, his hand was a blur.

"Give us some of the gold," said Maxie. "If you do, I'll drop out of the Tall Tale Contest."

"Maxie, you're such a nice guy," said Billy. "If you drop out, then the Meatballs will get the tickets to Paul Bunyan Land."

Darryl looked up. "We don't need any tickets," he said. "As soon as I get the gold, I'm going to buy Paul Bunyan Land."

"Great," said Billy. "Then that means we'll all get in for free."

"Nope. It means you're not going to get in at all," said Darryl. He scooped up another handful of bones and tossed them out of the pit.

"Yuck!" said Homer, turning away.

"Hey, what's that?" said Maxie, walking over to the pile of bones.

Homer turned. Maxie was poking the jumble of bones with a stick.

"Very interesting," said Maxie.

"Hey! Leave that stuff alone," said Homer, putting his hands on his hips. "Everything we dug up is ours. Finders keepers."

Maxie ignored Homer. He fished a crumpled-up piece of paper from the pile of bones and smoothed it out on the sand.

"If that's a map, you'd better hand it over," said Darryl, popping out of the pit. "Everything in this hole belongs to us."

"Everything!" said Homer, pointing.

"You can have it," said Maxie. He tossed the paper to Darryl and laughed. "It's not a map. It's a napkin, from Chipper's Rib Shack!"

Darryl picked up the napkin and turned it slowly over in his hands. "I don't get it," he said.

"Maybe Captain Golden Guts ate at Chipper's before he died," said Homer. "My uncle says the food there is awful."

Maxie rolled his eyes. "Chipper's wasn't around in the days of the pirates," he said. "Neither was the town."

Darryl glanced back at the hole. Under

the sand he could see more paper, some bags, and two plastic cups.

"You didn't find Golden Guts. You found the leftovers from a picnic," said Maxie.

Darryl reached into the sand and dug out the bag.

CHIPPER'S RIB SHACK. RIBS THAT STICK TO YOUR RIBS. CHIPPER REAVES, PROPRIETOR, it said on the sack.

Darryl wadded up the bag and threw it on the sand. "Rats!"

"Rats is right," said Maxie. "You're going to have a ton of them unless you clean up this mess."

"What mess?" said Darryl.

"All this litter," said Maxie. He snapped his suspenders and grinned. "You can't leave all these bones and paper on the beach. It's against the law."

"Clean it up! Clean it up!" chanted the Jokers, pointing.

"Dump it in the trash," said Maxie. He pointed to some barrels at the edge of the parking lot. "Do a good job and we won't report you."

"Report me? For what? This stuff isn't mine," said Darryl.

"That isn't what you said a minute ago," said Billy, picking at his teeth with his little finger. "You said everything in the hole is yours."

Darryl sighed. Homer too.

"It's the law," said Maxie. "No littering."

Darryl glanced at the trash, then up at the Jokers.

"You'd better clean up or we'll call the police," said Billy.

The Jokers smiled. It looked as if they'd enjoy telling the police about the Meatballs.

Darryl growled.

"Go on," said Maxie.

"I guess someone better clean up," said Darryl, picking up the bag. He raised an eyebrow and looked at Maxie. "Especially with so many pigs running around."

The Jokers didn't think Darryl's joke was funny. Neither did Homer. He scooped up some napkins and a plastic cup. "You get me in more trouble," he said, starting for the trash cans.

"Don't get mad at me," said Darryl, hurrying alongside. "I was just trying to get you to Paul Bunyan Land so you could ride the merry-go-round with Molly."

"Well, you did an awful job of it," said Homer. "Instead of sending me to the park with Molly you sent me to the dump with a load of garbage."

CHAPTER 6

Coach Homer

ON THURSDAY morning Darryl put on an inside-out T-shirt and a pair of new white pants and headed for school. As usual he stopped at Ruby's Donuts for a bag of donut holes.

As usual he didn't find the ruby.

"Rats!" he said, feeding bits of donut to the pigeons on the sidewalk. "You think I would get lucky. Just once."

When the donuts were gone, he sighed and trudged off to school.

It was a beautiful day. Yellow sunshine painted the streets. Birds chirped happily in the trees. And the sweet smell of dewy grass filled the air with the promise of springtime. But Darryl didn't notice.

All he could think about was the Tall Tale Contest. How he was too afraid to speak. And how he was letting down his best friends, the Meatballs.

By the time he got to school, class had already begun.

Homer was standing in front of the class, practicing a tall tale.

". . . . so Mr. Wide-Awake never slept. He didn't even have a bed!"

Everyone clapped politely. Homer took a big bow.

"That was a very nice tall tale," said Mr. Foster.

"I thought it was very dumb," said

56

Molly, as Darryl came by, heading for his desk.

"It sounded okay to me," said Darryl, stopping.

"I wasn't talking to you," said Molly. She looked under her desk at her pretend poodle. "I was talking to Godzilla."

"Homer doesn't stand a chance tomorrow morning," she said, babbling on to her make-believe mutt. "Only Darryl can win us those tickets."

Darryl slid into his seat and lowered his head.

"Darryl, have you heard the good news?" asked Mr. Foster.

Darryl looked up. His face brightened. "Is the contest called off?"

"No, of course not," said Mr. Foster. "The good news is that we get to rehearse our tall tales in the auditorium. Right after lunch."

"We do?" said Darryl.

58

"You can tell us about the time you took a ride on a flying saucer," said Mr. Foster. "Best of all, only our class will be there, so you won't have to be afraid of talking to strangers."

"I don't know," said Darryl. He dried his sweaty hands on his white pants and scrunched down in his seat. "Do I have to?"

"You ought to at least try," said Mr. Foster. "The class really wants those tickets."

"Please," said Homer. "I can be your coach." He turned and gave Molly a little wave. "My valentine and I are counting on it."

Molly rolled her eyes.

"Meatballs help each other," said Kate. She touched the freckle at the tip of her nose. "That's one of our main rules."

Darryl clenched his teeth and groaned. After what seemed like forever he moaned and said, "Okay, I'll try. If I have to."

Everyone clapped.

"We're on our way to Paul Bunyan Land!" said Luis.

I wish I were on my way to Mars, thought Darryl.

CHAPTER 7

Pizza Talk

DARRYL FELT sick the rest of the morning. Every time he'd think about giving his speech, his face would turn as pale as his pants.

At lunch he wasn't any better.

"Eat your pizza," said Homer, leaning across the table. "You can't give a speech if you're hungry. Eat. That's an order from your coach."

"I don't need a coach," said Darryl.

"Everyone needs a coach," said Homer. He tapped Darryl on the nose. "Now do as I say, eat!"

Darryl couldn't. He was too nervous. Just the thought of food made his stomach start to twitch.

"You're making a big mistake," said Homer, waving his own floppy pizza in Darryl's face. "If you don't eat, you might faint in the middle of your tall tale." He smiled. "If that happened, my valentine and I couldn't ride the merry-go-round."

Just then the bell rang.

"It's time!" said Homer, jumping up.

Darryl gulped.

"I'll bring your pizza," said Homer, picking it up. "Maybe you'll get hungry later."

Darryl got up slowly. His legs felt shaky. His head felt hazy. "I've got a bad feeling about this," he muttered.

Everyone met in the auditorium. Homer

and Darryl took chairs on the lighted stage. The rest of the class sat in the darkened auditorium.

"Since I'm Darryl's coach, I'm going to see that he gets the right food," said Homer, waving the pizza.

"Food is important," said Mr. Foster. "But I'm not sure that he needs pizza. A banana would be healthier."

"What if I mashed a banana onto the pizza?" suggested Homer. "That way he'd get a little bit of everything." Homer closed his eyes. "Mmmmm. A banana pizza. I can almost smell it now."

Darryl popped Homer on the shoulder. "What's wrong with you? Do you want to make me sick?"

Homer shook his head.

Darryl sighed and peered out into the gloom. "There's nobody else here, is there?"

"Only your friends," called Mr. Foster from the darkness. "Please. Go ahead."

Darryl took a deep breath and walked to the microphone. Homer put the pizza on Darryl's empty chair and sat down in another one to listen.

"If you change your mind, your pizza is waiting," he said, patting the chair.

Darryl gripped the microphone and squinted out at the class. "Do I have to?" he said.

"Yes!" everyone shouted back.

Darryl sighed, then took a deep breath. Finally, in what was little more than a whisper, he began to speak. "I'm going to tell a tall tale about . . . umm . . . ummm . . ." He made a face and tightened his hands around the microphone. "Umm . . . the tall tale is . . . about . . . umma . . . umma . . ."

"About the time you took a ride in a flying saucer," shouted Mr. Foster, helping out.

"That's right," said Darryl. "I was sitting

64

under a tree by the river when—when . . ."

"When some aliens with antennas on their heads and big green eyes came walking up!" whispered Homer.

"Right," said Darryl. He looked around for the exit. "Then after that I umm . . . ummm . . ."

"Got zapped in the head!" yelled Molly.

"Right!" said Darryl. His face was red and sweaty.

"They carried me inside their saucer," shouted Luis.

"Yes, they did," said Darryl. "They told me they were from—from . . ."

"Mars!" shouted Kate.

"Yes!" said Darryl. "Then—then. Then I escaped and ran home. The end!"

"Hooray!" shouted Luis.

"Great story!" said Mr. Foster.

"Really?" said Darryl. He smiled. "Really? You liked it?"

"I loved it," said Mr. Foster.

"You were great," said Homer, when Darryl returned to his chair. "See? That was easy."

Darryl grinned and raised his arms. "Hey! I can do it!" he said. "Maxie better watch out now."

Everyone clapped harder than ever. Darryl felt warm all over. He waved again and sat down.

"Look out!" screamed Homer.

KER-SQUISH! Darryl sank into the pizza.

"Eee-yew. What was that?" asked Darryl, afraid of what the answer might be.

"Whoopsie," said Homer, forcing a smile.

Darryl stood up and slowly turned around.

The slice of pizza hung for a moment on the back of his white pants. Then, slow as a slug, the crust slid off and flopped onto

the floor, leaving behind a gooey glob of cheese and tomato sauce.

"Yuck. That's so sick," said someone in the back of the auditorium. "Gross!"

No one had to guess who it was. No one but Maxie Butts hissed out his *s*'s.

"You should have worn a diaper!" he shouted.

A roar of laughter came rolling out of the darkness. It sounded like the whole Joker gang was back there.

Darryl's face turned as red as the tomato sauce dripping from his pants.

"Nice speech!" yelled a Joker.

"Nice pants!" shouted another.

"Hurry up with that diaper!" cried Maxie.

Darryl's face went from red to purple.

"I'm really sorry," said Homer, patting him on the back.

Darryl lowered his head. "I knew I shouldn't have tried to speak," he said. "It's just like kindergarten all over again."

"No, it's not," said Homer, giving Darryl's shoulder a hug.

"You're right," said Darryl, putting his hands to his face. "It's worse!"

"Maxie Butts! Look at what you've done," said Mr. Foster. He jumped up and turned on the lights, but the Jokers had left. They'd slid out the back door. Off in the distance you could hear them, though, laughing down the hall.

"Accidents happen," said Mr. Foster, turning back to the stage. "Don't let those Jokers upset you. They only want you to drop out."

"Well, they just got their wish," said Darryl. "I quit."

"But you can't," said Homer, clasping his hands together, begging. "I was counting on you to put me and my valentine onto that merry-go-round."

"And I was counting on you," said Darryl. "Some coach!"

Homer got out his comb. "Gee. Sorry,"

he said, nervously combing his hair. "I just wanted to make you look good."

"You did a great job, didn't you?" said Darryl, as another blob of pizza plopped off his pants.

CHAPTER 8

Bad Dreams

DARRYL BARELY slept Thursday night. Every time he closed his eyes he saw Maxie laughing and pointing.

"I'll never give a speech again," he said, staring at the ceiling. "Never ever."

When at last Friday morning came, Darryl got up and went down to breakfast.

"What are you going to do at school today?" asked Darryl's father. Mr. Pumpwater was wearing an inside-out robe. His hair was standing up as if he'd been shocked. "Isn't this the morning of the Tall Tale Contest?"

Darryl nodded and played with his oatmeal.

"Eat a good meal," said Mr. Pumpwater. "You don't want to speak on an empty stomach."

Darryl took a bite of his cereal.

"I'm sure you'll give a great speech," said Mr. Pumpwater.

Darryl didn't say anything. He didn't want to tell his father that he had dropped out of the contest. More importantly, he didn't want to tell him that he wasn't even going to school that day. He couldn't face Maxie or the Jokers, or even the Meatballs.

He'd leave the house, but he wouldn't go to school. He'd go somewhere, anywhere, else. Probably China.

CHAPTER 9

The Thief

DARRYL WAS sorry he hadn't paid more attention in geography class. He had no idea where China was. He hoped it wasn't a long walk.

Before he went anywhere, though, he first had to visit Ruby's Donuts.

"You're late for school," said the owner, Mr. Chamberlain, handing Darryl a bag of donut holes. "It started five minutes ago."

"My new school starts later," said Darryl.

"What new school?" asked Mr. Chamberlain.

"China Elementary," said Darryl. "They're in a different time zone."

"You tell the wildest stories," said Mr. Chamberlain, scratching at his short black hair. He laughed. "You should enter a tall tale contest someday."

"Sure. Someday," said Darryl, heading out the door.

When Darryl got outside he was greeted by a mob of pigeons. They swirled about his feet, begging for crumbs.

"Everyone is probably at the tall tale assembly," he said, tossing donut holes to the pigeons. He looked down the street at Bayview School and sighed. "I'm going to miss that place. Especially the Meatballs."

Darryl took his time feeding the birds. He wasn't in a hurry.

"This is the last meal you guys are going

to get from me," he said, turning over the bag and shaking out the rest of the donut holes. "So you'd better enjoy it."

The donut chunks landed like heavy raindrops. *Pat! Pat! Pat! Pat! CLINK!*

"Clink?" said Darryl. He squinted into the swirl of pigeons fighting over the crumbs. "What kind of a donut goes clink?"

He bent over. Then gasped.

"Oh . . . oh . . . oh, my!" he cried, putting his hand to his mouth. "It's the Valentine's ruby!"

Lying on the sidewalk, blinking up at him like a big red eye, was the prize he'd been trying to win all year.

"I—I found it!" he yelled, doing a little dance. "Wowie cowie! I'm rich! Now I can buy Paul Bunyan Land! Now I can send Maxie to the South Pole!"

While Darryl was jumping up and clicking his heels, one of the pigeons walked

over, gave the ruby a peck, and picked it up.

"Hey!" yelled Darryl. "What are you doing?"

The pigeon gave Darryl a curious look, then began to hop away.

"Whoa! Come back here!"

The pigeon turned again, then flapped his wings.

"No! Don't fly away!" Without thinking twice, Darryl dived for the pigeon.

The bird didn't think twice either. He took off.

KA-BLAM! Darryl belly-flopped onto the sidewalk.

"Oooof!"

The rest of the birds scattered. Flapping and cooing, they rose up into the sky like a white tornado. For a moment they swirled above Main Street. Then, with the pigeon holding the ruby leading the way, they wheeled about and headed north.

"Come back here!" yelled Darryl, leaping to his feet. "Help! Police! I've been robbed!"

Darryl looked about desperately. The pigeons would soon be out of sight. And so would his dreams of riches.

Main Street was deserted. There wasn't a policeman around. Not even a dogcatcher. And his friends were all in school.

"The school!" he said, snapping his fingers. "That's it! I'll get the Meatballs."

CHAPTER 10

Help!

DARRYL FLEW down Main Street.

"I can't let that thief get away," he said, his arms pumping. "I've got to get a pigeon posse together. And fast!"

Darryl dashed up the stairs and into the Bayview School. Huffing and puffing he ran down the empty hallway.

"Help!" he cried, banging on all the

classroom doors. "The ruby is getting away!"

But no one came out. Darryl stopped for a moment and looked around, fighting to catch his breath.

Suddenly he heard a familiar voice come floating down the hallway. "And that's why he's called Captain Golden Guts!"

"It's Maxie!" said Darryl, heading for the auditorium. "So that's where everyone is."

The auditorium doors were open. Up onstage Maxie was standing in the spotlight with his arms raised over his head. "The story of Golden Guts is the greatest tall tale in Bayview!" he bragged. "The Jokers and I are happy to bring it to you."

Everyone was clapping. Billy Tubbs and the rest of the Jokers were in the first row. They stood up and gave Maxie a standing ovation.

Darryl rubbed his hands together nervously and searched the darkened room for the Meatballs.

"This is horrible, horrible," he muttered. "Every minute that goes by, that pigeon gets farther away."

Up onstage Mr. Walker, the principal, was introducing the last tall tale contestant.

"Now let's hear the story of the man who didn't own a bed. Here to tell us all about Mr. Wide-Awake is Homer King!"

"Homer!" shouted Darryl, just as Homer stepped up to the microphone.

Homer waved. In his too-big polka-dot shirt and floppy striped pants he looked a little like a tall tale himself: Mister Funny Clothes. While everyone was waiting for him to begin he started to comb his hair.

"Homer, go ahead!" Mr. Foster called out from somewhere in the crowd. "Everyone is waiting."

Homer cleared his throat. But before he

could begin, Darryl came dashing onto the stage.

"Homer!" he yelled, running over and grabbing his friend by both shoulders. "Help!"

"Huh?" said Homer.

"It's the ruby!" shouted Darryl. "I found it!"

"The ruby from Ruby's Donuts?" said Homer. "Wow! Kate said the odds on finding it were two million to one!"

"Sit down, you Meatball!" shouted Billy Tubbs from the front row. "You're holding up the show."

"Yeah!" yelled another Joker. "Maxie wants those tickets."

Darryl let go of Homer and squinted out at the crowd.

"It's true!" he said. "I found the ruby. This morning. While I was on my way to China."

Everyone laughed.

"You're such a liar!" shouted Billy.

Darryl shook his head. "I'm not lying this time. I really did find it."

"All right, then, let's see it!" yelled Maxie, from the side of the stage. "Go on. Show it to us."

Darryl lowered his head. "I can't," he mumbled. "That's why I came back here. I need everyone's help."

"What's this about?" asked Mr. Walker. The spotlight gleamed off his bald head as he strode back onto the stage.

"What kind of help do you need?" asked Homer. He looked around nervously and combed his hair. "Is someone after you?"

Darryl licked at his lips and looked about frantically. "We're wasting time," he said. "The thief is getting away!"

"Thief!" said Homer, whipping about. "Where? Where!"

"He's not here. He's in the air. Somewhere," said Darryl. He turned and faced the audience. "This morning, while I was walking to China, I stopped to buy some donut holes at Ruby's. When I got outside a big flock of pigeons was waiting for me. I started throwing them the donut crumbs when suddenly, *clink!* the Valentine ruby landed on the sidewalk."

"Really? How'd it get there?" asked Homer.

Darryl clapped a hand to the side of his head. "Stupid me! I'd thrown it to them accidentally."

"What happened then?" asked Homer. Everyone in the crowd leaned forward expectantly.

"One of the pigeons picked up the ruby. Before I could grab it, he flew away."

"Incredible!" said Homer.

"Incredible, but true," said Darryl. He pointed toward the back of the auditorium. "He's headed north. Maybe we can catch him yet."

"Wow!" said Homer. "That pigeon must be the richest bird in the world!"

Mr. Walker clapped. "Darryl, that was a

wonderful story. I've heard lots of tall tales in my life, but never any about the world's richest bird."

"But it's not a story," said Darryl, turning to the principal. "It's a hundred percent true."

Mr. Walker clapped again. "A tall tale on top of a tall tale!"

Darryl turned back to the audience. "Doesn't anyone believe me? I'm serious. While on my way to China I really did beat two-million-to-one odds and find that ruby. And a pigeon really did fly away with it."

The audience burst into applause.

"What a story!" one of the teachers yelled.

"What a speech!" shouted Kate Barnett.

Mr. Foster took a banana out of his pocket. "I think Darryl just earned himself a special treat," he said. "He told that story perfectly."

"And he didn't seem at all nervous," said Luis.

"How did he do it?" said Molly.

"But I'm serious!" said Darryl into the microphone. "We have to organize a pigeon posse and track down that bird. What if he drops the ruby into a lake? A fish might eat it!"

Everyone laughed. Then applauded louder than ever.

CHAPTER 11

The Champion

DARRYL SHOOK his head. It was hopeless. No one believed him.

Suddenly, Maxie Butts came stomping out onstage and smacked him on the shoulder.

"I thought you were supposed to be too scared to speak," he said. "Or was that just a tall tale too?"

"Tall tale?" said Darryl.

"Yeah, like you just told for the contest," said Maxie. He snarled and popped Darryl on the shoulder again. "I thought you still remembered what I did to you in kindergarten."

Darryl wrinkled up his nose. "Kindergarten? Tall tale?"

"Congratulations to Darryl Pumpwater," said Mr. Walker, grabbing the microphone. "The judges have just voted. His amazing story wins this year's Tall Tale Contest."

"He won!" shouted Molly, from somewhere in the audience.

"I won?" said Darryl.

"You won!" shouted Homer, giving him a hug. "I'm on my way to the merry-go-round!"

Everyone in the auditorium was clapping and stomping their feet. Everyone but the Jokers. They were wadding up bits of paper and throwing them onto the stage.

"Those Meatballs are such cheaters," said one of the Jokers.

"He probably read that story in a book," said Billy Tubbs. "Nobody could make up a tall tale that good."

Darryl bowed to the crowd. "I won!" he said. "I did it!"

Suddenly the stage was flooded with Meatballs.

"I knew you wouldn't let your friends down," said Molly. She pushed her invisible poodle into Darryl's face. "Lucky you. You get a kiss from Godzilla."

Darryl made a face and wiped the invisible slime from his mouth.

Maxie growled for one last time and shuffled off the stage, mumbling to himself, "How does that guy dream up such great stories?"

The lights came on in the auditorium. Everyone got up and started heading back to class.

Darryl looked out at the crowd. "Wow. Did I really just speak in front of all those people?"

"You were terrific," said Homer. He patted his chest. "Of course, I knew you could do it all along. That's probably what makes me such a great coach."

"I can hardly wait to go to Paul Bunyan Land," said Molly.

"Me too," said Homer. He swallowed hard, then drew in a deep breath. "Molly, will you be my valentine and go on a ride with me at Paul Bunyan Land?"

Molly lowered her head, then looked up and smiled. "I'd love to," she said.

Homer grinned and leapt a foot off the ground. "Really? You will?"

"There's a ride there I've wanted to go on for years," she said.

"The merry-go-round?" asked Homer.

"No, silly. That's a baby ride," said Molly. "You and I are going on the Tornado

Twister. I've heard it will turn your stomach inside out."

"It will?" said Homer, grabbing his stomach. For a moment it looked like he might get sick.

"We're going to have so much fun!" said Molly.

Homer moaned and reached for his comb.

Just then Mr. Foster handed Darryl a banana. "You've earned this," he said. "That was the wildest story I've ever heard. You've got a terrific imagination."

Darryl gave the banana back. "You deserve this. Not me," he said. "You told the tallest tale today. Just now."

"What tall tale did I tell?" asked Mr. Foster.

"You said my story was made up. But that's just it. It wasn't!"

Mr. Foster smiled. So did all the Meatballs.

94

"You can't stop, can you?" said Luis.

"Next he'll tell us he found Captain Golden Guts," said Kate.

"Or that the Martians just landed outside," said Nicole.

Darryl sighed and shook his head. It was hopeless. No one was ever going to believe him. But he really didn't care. He'd just won the greatest prize of all. Thanks to the ruby, he was no longer afraid of Maxie. And no longer afraid of speaking either.

"You've got a great future as a speaker," said Homer. "Next month I'll help you run for school president."

Darryl grinned. "I think I'd like that."

"Then after that it's going to be mayor. Then governor." Homer raised his fist. "There's going to be no stopping you!"

Darryl gripped the collar of his inside-out shirt and raised his head high. "Why, I bet a good speaker like me could even be President someday."

"I bet you could," said Homer.

Darryl beamed. President!

Suddenly anything seemed possible. And this time everyone knew it was no tall tale.

FIVE FREAKY SPORTS FACTS

The footbow is shot while lying on your back and pushing out the wooden part of the bow with your feet. Harry Drake of Lakeside, California, holds the distance record. In October of 1979 he shot an arrow over three fourths of a mile!

Fred Lorz crossed the finish line first in the 1904 Olympic marathon. But his medal was taken away when it turned out he only ran 15 of the 26 miles. He rode in a car the rest of the way!

Hockey player Phil Watson once said to reporters, "Gentlemen, I have nothing to say. Any questions?"

The shortest baseball player ever to play in a major-league game was Eddie Gaedel. He was only three feet seven inches tall. He was only up to bat once, on August 19, 1951. He crouched low and the pitcher couldn't pitch a strike. He walked on four straight balls. His number? 1/8.

In a 1968 baseball game Gates Brown, a pinch hitter for the Detroit Tigers, was suddenly called up to bat. Gates had just sneaked two hot dogs into the dugout for a snack. He stashed the hot dogs under his shirt and went up to bat. He hit a double and had to slide into second on his stomach. When he stood up, the front of his shirt was stained with mustard, and the hot dogs and buns were leaking onto the base.

The Meatballs monkey around in
ALL-STAR MEATBALLS #8

April Fools

The All-Star Meatballs become superspies to find out what happened to Mr. Foster. He's been absent since Monday, and Luis Cruzon says he saw a lion biting Mr. Foster's head off in the circus parade. Now Luis has to persuade the principal, Mr. Walker, to let him walk the tightrope in circus tryouts so the Meatballs can find out what happened to their teacher from behind the scenes.

SOUP RIDES AGAIN!

Whether he's riding into trouble on horseback or rolling into trouble on an outrageous set of wheels, Soup and his best friend Rob have a knack for the kind of crazy mix-ups that are guaranteed to make you laugh out loud!

☐ SOUP 48186-4 $3.25
☐ SOUP FOR PRESIDENT 48188-0 $3.25
☐ SOUP IN THE SADDLE 40032-5 $3.25
☐ SOUP ON FIRE 40193-3 $3.25
☐ SOUP ON ICE 40115-1 $2.99
☐ SOUP'S DRUM 40003-1 $2.95
☐ SOUP'S GOAT 40130-5 $2.95
☐ SOUP'S UNCLE 40308-1 $2.95
☐ SOUP IN LOVE 40755-9 $3.25
☐ SOUP'S HOOP 40589-0 $3.25

At your local bookstore or use this handy page for ordering:

DELL READERS SERVICE, DEPT. DRN
2451 South Wolf Road, Des Plaines, IL. 60018
Please send me the above title(s). I am enclosing $ _____.
(Please add $2.50 per order to cover shipping and handling.) Send check or money order—no cash or C.O.D.s please.

Ms./Mrs./Mr _____

Address _____

City/State _____ Zip_____

DRN–2/93

Prices and availability subject to change without notice. Please allow four to six weeks for delivery.